A SOLVE-THE-STORY PUZZLE ADVENTURE

PUZZLOO!ES

THE MUSEUM OF SUPERNATURAL HISTORY

MW00945343

BY RUSSELL GINNS AND JONATHAN MAIER

ILLUSTRATED BY KRISTEN TERRANA-HOLLIS

Copyright © 2021 by Random House Children's Books

All rights reserved. Published in the United States by Random House Children's Books, a division of Penguin Random House LLC, New York.

Random House and the colophon are registered trademarks of Penguin Random House LLC.

Visit us on the web! **rhcbooks.com**
For a variety of teaching tools, educators and librarians can visit us at **RHTeachersLibrarians.com**.

ISBN: 978-0-525-57213-8 (trade paperback)

Cover design by Igor Jovicic
Cover art and interior illustration by Kristen Terrana-Hollis
Interior design by Peter Leonardo

Printed in the United States of America

10 9 8 7 6 5 4 3 2 1

First Edition

Random House Children's Books supports the First Amendment and celebrates the right to read.

What's a Puzzlooey?

Puzzlooies are stories you read by solving puzzles.

They're smart, surprising, and seriously silly.

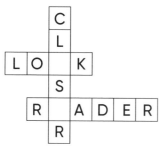

Each amazing adventure is chock-full of challenges, perplexing pictures, and mysterious messages. Plus there's always an extra helping of hilarious jokes and fascinating facts!

Let these zany, brainy kids introduce you to the story. They might even help with a clue or two. Start reading and puzzling. It's all up to you!

Eunice   **Maralee**

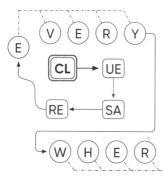

Ray   **Clinton**

How to Solve This Story

DETAIL DETECTOR

Every Puzzlooey is told through a mix of chapters and puzzles. To solve it all, you'll have to pay attention to many of the things you discover along the way.

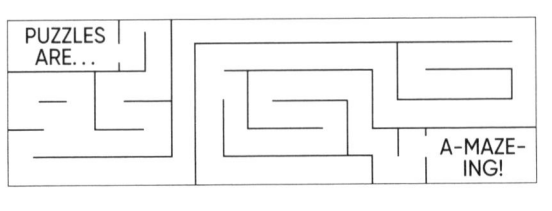

PUZZLES ARE...

A-MAZE-ING!

CLUE COLLECTOR

You'll need a few things to make the most of this book:
- A pencil
- Scissors
- A ruler

PUZZLER PROPS

HINT: READ THE FIRST LETTER OF EACH BOLD WORD

Most of all, you'll need to use your **baloney radiator and impossible necktie.**

(Psst: Don't skip ahead before solving a puzzle.)

The Museum Is Open!

Zombie our guest! This story is **exhibit**-ing a sense of danger. **Creep** an eye out for signs of trouble.

The excitement is *building*, that's for sure!

Solving this story will take all your **skulls**, talents, and a keen sense of **spell**.

So get in line for...

THE MUSEUM OF SUPERNATURAL HISTORY

 U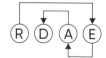

U R 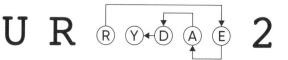 2

YETI OR NOT, HERE WE COME!

"I changed my mind," Chad Stoker said and stopped in his tracks. "I don't want to go in there."

Jayden Poe couldn't believe it. They had changed buses seven times, waited twenty-five minutes for a drawbridge, then walked three miles to reach the place. The Supernatural History Museum was finally in sight, and *now* his friend was backing out?

Jayden tugged on Chad's arm.

"We don't have to stay long," he said, trying to keep things positive.

"It's too creepy," Chad replied, pulling himself loose.

"Oh come on," Jayden insisted. "It's gonna be hilarious. Like that movie we watched last week— *Invasion of the Zombie Lemurs from Mars.*"

"That movie was way too scary," Chad pointed out. "I turned it off after five minutes, remember?"

Jayden remembered.

His best friend was always getting scared, or queasy, or worried that the substitute gym teacher was a robot. Last month, Chad ruined the school trip to the botanical gardens. He insisted he saw a tyrannosaurus in the bushes. It caused a panic. The trip ended early.

But he wasn't going to let his friend change today's plan.

Chad had a gift certificate. He'd received it for his eleventh birthday: one hundred dollars to spend at the Supernatural History Museum! Jayden had finally convinced Chad to use it—*on the last day before the certificate expired.*

"How about this?" Jayden said. "We'll go right to the museum's cafeteria. It's called *The RestaurHaunt.* They have Supernatural Burgers. The buns glow in the dark! A hundred bucks gets us ten each. It'll be epic!"

Chad's mouth had fallen open.

"You're hungry, huh?" Jayden asked.

"Sta-a-a-rving," Chad answered, nodding slowly.

"Then let's go," said Jayden.

"Wait," said Chad. "My brain is having a debate with my stomach."

For a full minute, Chad stared out into space, not moving. Finally, he said, "Okay, stomach wins. But brain says we go right to the restaurant."

"Sure thing," Jayden said.

The boys agreed to save the certificate for food, and paid cash for the tickets at the museum entrance.

Inside, the main lobby was dominated by a hulking yeti standing on a frozen mountaintop.

"Look at him," Jayden said. "Phony as a three-dollar bill. Fake with a capital *F.* Pretend like a plastic…"

"I'm not looking," Chad said, staring at his own feet. "Which way to the Supernatural Burgers?"

"I can help with that," a voice called behind them.

Jayden turned to find a woman about his mom's age. She had a kind face and a hairstyle about two stories tall. She wore a badge that read, "Director Shelley."

"I'm in charge of this museum," she told them. "The RestaurHaunt is to your left, boys. But why not join my tour first?"

"Sorry, ma'am," Chad said. "That's not really our thing. We're just here for the Restaur—"

"A tour would be great," Jayden interrupted. "But, you should know, my friend is kinda scared."

"Nothing to be afraid of," Director Shelley said. "The museum is educational. It's the history of mystery with only a speck of spooky. You'll be safe with me."

Jayden didn't know if it was her gentle smile or soothing voice, but something got through to his friend.

"I guess so," Chad said with a shrug.

Director Shelley led them back to the yeti. "This creature lives high in the Himalaya mountains," she said. "You may know its other name."

With a ruler, use the stars as guides to draw five straight lines connecting each yeti pair. The leftover letters will answer this question:

WHAT'S ANOTHER NAME FOR A YETI?

"A yeti is also called an abominable snowman," said
Director Shelley. "Now follow me to the monster hall."
"Not looking," Chad announced, covering his eyes.

2 FEATURED CREATURES

Find all the creatures and mysterious things in this word search.
(There's a list on the back of this page.)
The leftover letters spell the first thing they see.

```
M   V   A   M   P   I   R   E
F   G   M   U   M   M   Y   P
L   I   A   N   F   R   D   O
O   A   S   I   H   O   R   L
W   N   B   C   M   O   A   A
E   T   R   O   L   L   G   K
R   A   N   R   L   S   O   C
E   N   T   N   E   B   N   A
W   T   S   O   H   G   R   J
```

LOOK HERE FOR LIST
OF SEARCH WORDS

SEARCH WORDS

BLOB	GIANT ANT	UFO
JACKALOPE	MUMMY	VAMPIRE
DRAGON	TROLL	WEREWOLF
GHOST	UNICORN	

They stopped at the marsh monster display. It was a woman covered in green scales and fins. Chad snuck a peek at it and immediately wished he hadn't.

Tilt this page back until you can read a word clearly.
Then, turn it sideways and tilt it to read another word.
They'll tell you what Chad saw.

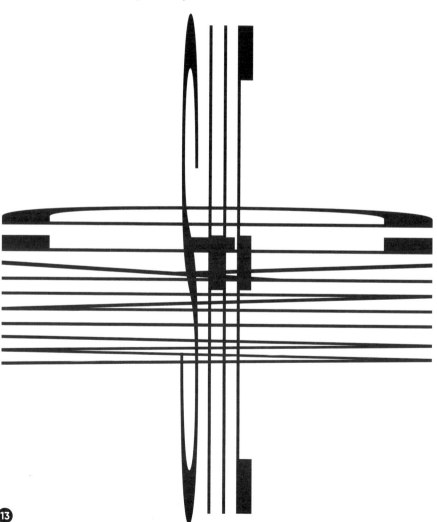

TERROR TOUR

"Did you see that?" Chad asked Jayden. "The marsh monster winked at us!"

"Ooo, something fishy is going on," Jayden joked. "It's just a trick. Probably done with motors."

"I don't know," Chad said, his voice quavering. "She sure seemed real."

Director Shelley came up behind them.

"That's our amphibious humanoid," she explained. The marsh monster lurks in wetlands where it eats insects and slugs...and chases nosy scientists."

Jayden glanced at Chad and rolled his eyes.

"Tell you what," he whispered. "I'll prove to you that everything here is completely fake. I'm going to have a few words with the woman in charge. Watch."

Before Jayden could speak with Director Shelley, however, she stepped quickly to the next exhibit and launched into another lecture.

"This is *not* a house plant," she said, gesturing to a tangle of leaves sprouting from two thick stalks. "It is a voracious Venezuelan vine-slinger. In deep jungles, it grows in the ground until the age of five. Then it yanks up its own roots and starts hunting in search of—shall I say—a hearty meal."

"Like a hamburger," Chad said wistfully.

"Or an eleven-year-old boy," Jayden said, nudging his friend toward the vine-slinger.

Chad twisted away. "Unfunny," he said.

Jayden sidled up next to Director Shelley.

"You don't *really* believe all this silly supernatural stuff, right?" he asked her.

"You mean everything in this museum?" she responded. "My life's work? The job I've poured myself into for years? Decades? Maybe even longer?"

"Uh, sorry," said Jayden. "I really didn't mean to…"

"Gotcha!" Director Shelley laughed. "I'm messing with you. All these exhibits are fake. It's all make-believe. For fun. Nothing's real. Not even the hamburger buns."

"I knew it!" Jayden exclaimed.

"Wait…what?" said Chad. "The buns?"

"Between you and me," said Director Shelley, leaning in toward them. "It's all a show for selling tickets."

She looked around.

"Or at least it used to be that way," she sighed. "We don't sell many tickets anymore. It's the location, I suppose. Not easy to get to."

"Oh, *we* know," Jayden said. "Seven buses and a drawbridge."

Director Shelley stared at the ceiling for an uncomfortable number of seconds.

"We'll need to shut down soon," she said. "Very soon."

Jayden didn't know what to say to that, so he silently shuffled backward until he was standing next to Chad again.

"Listen up, Stoker," he told him. "It's all phony. The director just admitted it. So you can stop worrying."

"I'm not so sure," Chad answered. "It's still a big creep-fest. And I've got a bad feeling there's something up with this whole place."

Jayden ignored him.

"You know what?" he said. "Director Shelley spends all day lying to people and taking their money, but I feel sad for her. She's talking about closing the place down."

"I can live with that," Chad said. "Can we eat now?"

"Fine," Jayden said, exasperated. "Just let me look at a couple more—"

"See you at the RestaurHaunt," Chad cut him off. "Can't promise there will be food left for you."

He darted away, head down, not looking at a single exhibit.

When Jayden turned around, he found that the director had moved on. He stood alone in front of a portrait of a woman in some kind of uniform.

"Everybody's ditched me," he said to the painting.

The woman had a half-smile, as if keeping a secret. Her skin seemed to be lit from within.

Glow-in-the-dark paint, Jayden figured. *Cool effect.*

He stepped closer so he could check out an info card beside the frame.

The card read: ABIGAIL JACKSON, 1917–1954. The rest of the label was damaged, however.

Jayden studied the mixed-up words carefully.

Copy the letters on the seven tiles into the spaces at the bottom of this page. If you put them in the right order, they'll tell you more about Abigail Jackson.

	E I		G H		N U
	R S E				S H
	O S T				S

A

"Ghost nurse," said Jayden. "That's not so interesting."

But the card explained that this ghost had a very important role in the museum.

Use the guide at the bottom to decode this message.
It will tell you what a ghost nurse can cure.

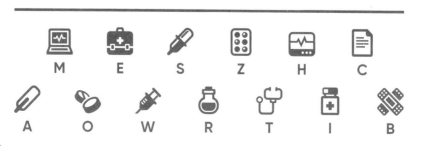

M	E	S	Z	H	C
A	O	W	R	T	I	B

"See ya, ghost nurse," Jayden said to the portrait. "If I ever get a vampire bite or something, I'll call you."

Then, as he turned to go, a movement caught his eye.

Start at the **A** and read every third letter.
Keep going until you get the answer to this question:

WHAT'S MOVING?

PLANT FOOD

Jayden reeled backward as the ghost nurse's hand reached for him. He fell on his butt, legs still kicking, and propelled himself another twenty feet before he stood up and tore out of the room.

He didn't stop until he reached Chad, who was already eating in the RestaurHaunt. His table was piled with Supernatural Burgers, bags of fries, and four jumbo-sized milkshakes. Jayden stood over his friend, sweating and out of breath.

Chad moved a giant bite of hamburger into his left cheek so he could talk.

"You look like you saw a ghost," he said, munching.

Jayden spoke between gasps for air, *"Ghost...nurse. Hand. Reach. Tried to...grab me!"*

"Nice try, Jayden," Chad said. "You deserve an acting award for..."

The rest of his words were muffled as he resumed chewing his hamburger.

Jayden slumped onto the bench next to Chad, dazed.

"Try one of these," Chad said, pushing a cup in front of Jayden. "They call them Mystery Milkshakes because you don't know what flavor you're gonna get. I think mine was banana-bacon-mint. *So-o-o good.*"

Jayden smiled despite what he was feeling.

There was so much awesome food.

He started thinking again about what he had seen— or what he *thought* he had seen: a ghost hand reaching out for him. It couldn't be real. It must've been a video projection, or something like that. And why should he care anyway? *They had all this awesome food!*

Jayden opened one of the Supernatural Burger bags. Inside—sure enough—the bun was glowing. He pulled it out and took a bite.

"De-liff-shush," he said through a full mouth.

The boys spent the next twenty glorious minutes stuffing their faces, not saying anything.

When he couldn't take another bite, Jayden wiped his lips with his sleeve.

"Let's take another look at that painting," he said.

"Really?" Chad asked. "I thought you made that up. Besides, the museum is closing soon."

"I really want to check it out," Jayden told him.

The room with the nurse portrait was empty. In fact, the boys seemed to be the last visitors left. While Chad stood nearby, staring at his feet, Jayden studied the painting. He couldn't see anything unusual. Next, he scanned the ceiling for a projector, but found nothing.

"Waste of time," Chad said. "Let's get out of here before they lock us in."

"Not so fast," a gruff, watery voice said.

Startled, the boys whirled around. In the middle of the room stood the vine-slinger and, next to him, the marsh monster!

Chad gasped and started to bolt, but Jayden snagged him by the collar.

"Hold on," Jayden said. "They can't be real."

The woman stretched her swampy arms and neck. Her scales rippled and shimmered.

"It's dreadful, striking a pose all day," she told them.

"They t-talk," Chad whimpered.

"Relax. They're just actors," Jayden said, trying to convince himself as much as Chad. "They're all wearing costumes."

"Costumes?" the plant man grumbled. He glanced at the marsh monster. "Can you believe the nerve of this kid?"

"Don't get your roots in a twist, dear Shrubley," she said. "We need them."

"Totally fake," Jayden said to Chad. "Watch."

He slid next to the plant man, grasped one of the leaves sticking out of his head, and plucked it out.

"Youch!" howled the plant man. "That's my leaf!"

Jayden dropped the leaf, startled by how real that scream sounded.

Suddenly, a vine shot out from the plant man's arm and wrapped around Jayden's foot like a whip. The vine reeled the foot in. The monster chomped down hard on Jayden's ankle. A searing pain shot up Jayden's leg.

"How do *you* like it?" the plant man snapped.

The boys screamed together. Jayden pried the plant man's head away from his leg. But the vines still held his foot. He had to get loose!

EVERYTHING'S VINE

Cut out these nine squares along the dotted lines.
Arrange them so they form a 3 x 3 picture.
It's something Chad can do to get away.

As Jayden slipped out of his shoe, the painting of the nurse started rattling and knocking against the wall.

"Oh no! What's happening?" Chad wailed.

8 FRAME-US LAST WORDS

Start at the top-left arrow and read the letters as you go.
When you reach a new arrow, head in that direction.
The trail will spell what's happening.

START →	T	H	E	N	U	R	↓
↓	E	L	←	A	R	S	
W	B	D	↑	F	E	←	
F	↑	↓	N	←	Y	←	
R	P	→	T	I	N	G	
O	K	→	↓	A	I	↓	
M	I	H	E	P	O	V	
→	T	↑	→	↑	E	R	

"She came out of the frame!" shouted Jayden. "Run!"

"Museum monsters!" the ghost nurse called as she swooped across the room. "Get the boys!"

9 DANGER DASH

Avoid the monsters and find a path that leads to safety.

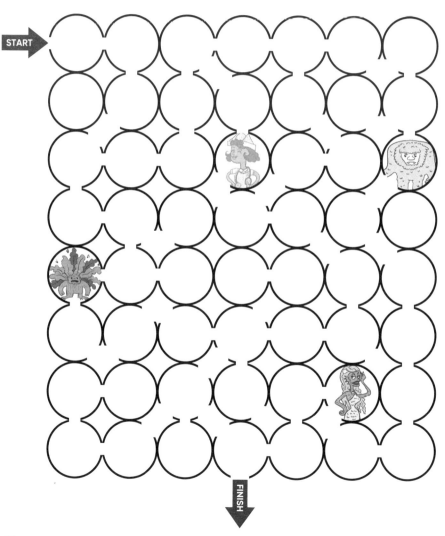

MONSTER MAYHEM

Jayden and Chad sprinted through the museum halls as monsters leapt from their exhibits and joined the chase—a werewolf, a vampire, a mummy, zombies, giant ants, a blob, a giant snake, and a dozen other strange creatures. Jayden's ankle throbbed.

The boys turned a corner to find a marble staircase to the next floor. They bounded up the steps three at a time. When they reached the top, Jayden saw a cylindrical trash can. He tipped it over and kicked it down the stairs. It collided with the rising tide of monsters.

"That'll buy us some time," Jayden said.

Down the hall, he spotted a door with a sign:

MECH. ROOM

"In there!" Jayden shouted, pointing at the door.

Inside the Mechanical Room, pipes crisscrossed the walls and ceiling. A bank of metal towers hummed in the middle of the room, their front panels filled with blinking buttons and dials. In the corner sat a metal desk, caked in dust, that looked as if it hadn't been used in a thousand years.

"Quick!" Jayden yelled. "Help me use the desk to block the door!"

The boys pushed and tugged the desk into place. It occurred to Jayden that it wouldn't do much good against a ghost nurse, but he kept that thought to himself.

Outside, the boys could hear the monsters grumbling. They stood motionless and held their breath. The expression on his friend's face worried Jayden. Chad's eyes were as big as the lenses of his glasses. His mouth was locked in the shape of a scream.

If only Jayden hadn't insisted they check out the painting, they wouldn't be here. (And his leg wouldn't have holes in it.) It was on him to make it right.

Posted on the back of the door was a map of the building, every room labeled. One of them caught Jayden's eye: the museum director's office on the same floor they were now on. He had an idea.

"Here's what we're going to do," he told Chad. "I'll go out there and lead the monsters back downstairs. When it's safe, you run to Director Shelley's office and tell her what's going on."

Chad mouthed the words *don't go.*

"They're gonna find us here sooner or later," said Jayden. "Then we'd both be done for. This is our best chance for survival."

Jayden didn't think he'd been very convincing, but Chad nodded slowly. They slid the table away from the door, and Jayden slipped outside.

He darted to the top of the stairs and yelled, "We're over here, you creeps!"

From every direction, monsters charged toward him. Jayden hopped onto the handrail and slid down the stairs in seconds.

Now, he thought, *just gotta keep them distracted until Chad can...*

A vine seized him by the shoulder.

"Who you calling creeps?" asked the plant man.

The marsh monster gripped his other arm in her slimy hands.

"Quite rude," she said, as they pulled Jayden through the museum. "We have names, you know—and *feelings*. I'm Marsha and this is Shrubley."

The pain in Jayden's leg flared up again. He was hobbling by the time the monsters returned him to the nurse's room.

"Jayden! Thank goodness!" the nurse exclaimed as she hovered in front of her empty painting. "I was worried we'd lost you."

She reached into the painting and withdrew a vial of glowing green liquid.

"We all need your help, dear boy," she said. "But first, there's something I have to do."

Nurse Jackson reached back into the painting. She fished around for a while and pulled out one more thing.

10 CURE GONNA GET IT

Use the list of things that Nurse Jackson has, and fit them all into this crossword. The letters in the shaded spaces will tell you what she is going to use.

Ice

Cake

Eggs

Fish

Soap

Paste

Shoes

Cheese

Stitches

"Wait!" Jayden shouted, struggling to break free. "What's she going to do with that shot?"

"There's no need to worry," Nurse Jackson said.

Start at JAB and make new words by changing one letter at a time. The first and last words will tell you what happens next.

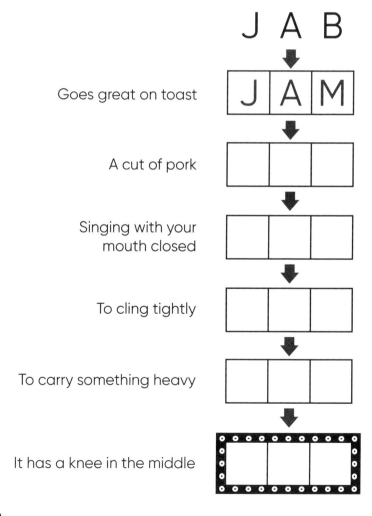

J A B

Goes great on toast — J A M

A cut of pork

Singing with your mouth closed

To cling tightly

To carry something heavy

It has a knee in the middle

Jayden felt the needle prick his leg with a small jab.
"See?" the nurse said. "That didn't hurt, did it?"
But Jayden couldn't answer.

12 SWIRLING THOUGHTS

Each cloud has one word in a circle.
Find the start of each one. The first letter of each word
will tell you what Jayden does next.

If it's a Puzzlooey, you know there's going to be an intermission. So take a break and relax, with some...

Amazing Facts

A Venus flytrap can count up to two! Its jaw-like leaf is covered in tiny hairs. When a bug lands on one of its hairs, the plant waits for it to touch a second hair. Then, the leaf snaps shut.

The author Mary Shelley wrote *Frankenstein* after another writer proposed a ghost story competition.

Dracula (from the story by Bram Stoker) is the most popular monster role in movies and TV. Over 90 actors have played the famous vampire.

A human skeleton consists of 206 bones. Each of your hands alone has 27 (one more bone than a foot has).

The Smithsonian Institution in Washington, D.C. is the largest museum complex in the world. If you looked at every object in the collection for just one minute, it would take you 296 years (without sleeping) to view it all.

The first person to scale Mt. Everest, Sir Edmund Hillary, searched for evidence of the yeti. In 1960, he found what he claimed was the creature's scalp. Scientists later figured out that the piece of hide was from a goat-like animal called a serow.

The American Museum of Natural History in New York has the largest meteorite on display anywhere. It weighs 15 tons.

Arthur Conan Doyle, the creator of Sherlock Holmes, believed in ghosts. He even belonged to a research group called The Ghost Club. The club also had another famous member: Charles Dickens, the writer of *A Christmas Carol*.

These are real museums around the world:
  Barbed Wire Museum (La Crosse, Kansas)
  Underwater Museum of Art (Cancun, Mexico)
  Museum of Miniature Books (Baku, Azerbaijan)
  Dog Collar Museum (Kent, England)
  Sulabh International Museum of Toilets
  (New Delhi, India)

While we're taking a break from Mr. Poe and Mr. Stoker, let's think like a joker! Here are some Puzzlooey-perfect...

Riddles and Jokes

Q: What do sea monsters eat for dinner?
A: Fish and ships.

Q: Why didn't the skeleton cross the road?
A: He didn't have the guts.

Q: What are a ghost's favorite foods?
A: Spook-ghetti, scare-ots, boo-berry pie, and I scream.

Q: What do you get when you cross a vampire and a snowman?
A: Frostbite.

Q: Why don't mummies take vacations?
A: They don't want to relax and unwind.

Q: What do you do if 30 zombies surround your house?
A: Hope that it's Halloween.

Q: Why didn't the skeleton go to the party?
A: He had no body to go with.

Q: What do you call a building filled with cow paintings?
A: A moo-seum.

Q: Where's a good place to see antlers?
A: A moose-eum.

Q: Are you allowed to take pictures at a museum?
A: No, they need to stay on the wall.

Q: How long can you stay at the clock museum?
A: Until you run out of time.

Knock Knock!
Who's there?
Fangs.
Fangs who?
Fangs for letting me in!

Knock Knock!
Who's there?
Ghost.
Ghost who?
Ghost stand somewhere else.

THE COSMIC PLUNGER ALIGNMENT

Jayden opened his eyes with the dim hope that it had all been a bad dream.

"There you are!" the nurse said in a sing-songy voice.

She waved from the end of a museum bench.

Nope. Not a dream.

Jayden lay on the other end of the bench. His head felt thick, but the stabbing pain in his ankle was gone. And somebody—or something—had returned his shoe to his foot.

The nurse patted his knee. It felt like drops of ice water.

"I fixed you right up with a little shot of Supernatural Serum," she said.

Jayden rolled back his sock and stared. His ankle was good as new.

"Thanks, I guess," he said. "But I'm not wild about strangers stabbing me with shots."

"Call me Nurse Jackson," she told him. "Now we're not strangers."

She turned away and called out, "Shrubley! Come here and apologize."

The carnivorous vine-slinger shambled over to the bench.

"Sorry I bit your ankle," he grumbled. "If it makes you feel any better, you've got a fine-tasting leg."

"I'm sorry, too," Jayden said. "Next time, I'll *leaf* well enough alone."

"Hah," Shrubley chuckled. "Good one."

Nurse Jackson's expression had turned serious.

"We need your help, Jayden," she said solemnly.

"*My* help?" he replied, glancing around the room filled with monsters. "Why don't you ask one of *them*?"

"I can explain," said the nurse. "We are being held captive here and forced to be on exhibit. An ancient mystical ruler cast a spell. It prevents us from leaving the museum.

She lowered her voice eerily.

"She is a flaming skeleton named…*Kazzerax*."

All the monsters murmured uneasily.

"Sounds like a bad rash," Jayden said.

Nurse Jackson continued, "We are all worried that Kazzerax is planning something catastrophic. The Cosmic Plunger Alignment is coming soon."

"Did you say, 'plunger'?" Jayden asked.

"Yes," Nurse Jackson said. "Every 154,267 years, planets and stars line up in the sky in the shape of a giant plunger. The Cosmic Plunger Alignment is an extraordinary supernatural event that creates unlimited mystical power. Those who know how to use it can harness that power for their own evil purposes."

She lowered her voice again.

"And Kazzerax knows how to do it," she whispered.

"Wait a minute," said Jayden. "Something called Kazzerax has magical janitor skills. And it's going to use some super-cosmic-plunger power."

"Yes, in a manner of speaking," Nurse Jackson answered. "And she must be stopped. Not just for our sakes. The whole world is in peril."

"But what am I going to do?" Jayden protested. "I've got no power. Look at my arms. They're noodles."

"We watched you today," the ghost nurse said. "You're not afraid. You're kind of spunky. And *you* are not bound to this building as we are."

"Why is that important?" Jayden asked.

"Whatever Kazzerax has planned will happen outside the building," she answered. "Beneath the Cosmic Plunger."

"I have an idea," Jayden said. "Ask Director Shelley for help. I bet she knows what to do."

The room went silent.

"Her human form is a disguise," said Nurse Jackson, shaking her head. "Director Shelley *is* Kazzerax."

"But I sent Chad to find her!" Jayden gasped.

Before anyone could stop him, Jayden rushed out of the room.

When Jayden arrived at Director Shelley's office, the room was empty. On her desk, he found a notepad with a strange symbol scrawled on it.

Use the guide at the bottom to fill in this grid. You'll draw what Jayden saw on the notepad.

■ = B2, B4, D7, E1, E2, E3, E4, E5, E6, E7, F7, H2, H4

▼ = G3, G5, I2, I4   ◤ = A2, A4, C3, C5

◢ = G2, G4, I1, I3, D6   ◣ = A1, A3, C2, C4, F6

	A	B	C	D	E	F	G	H	I
1									
2									
3									
4									
5									
6									
7									

Drawn on her whiteboard was a diagram of the Cosmic Plunger Alignment. Arrows pointed from the plunger to a spot on the museum grounds.

14 CAN M'YOU SEE 'EM?

Follow the path Jayden took through the museum. At the end of the path, you'll see where he wound up.

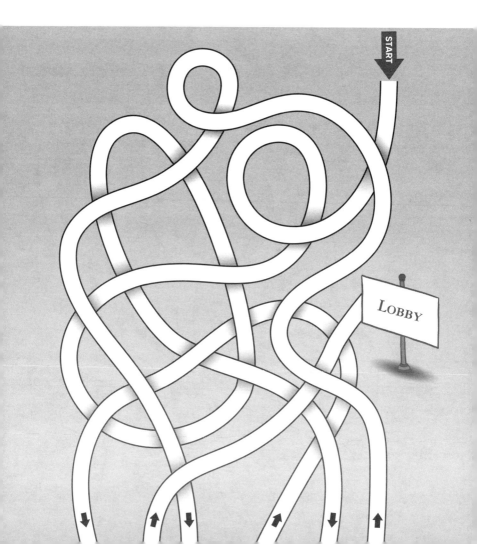

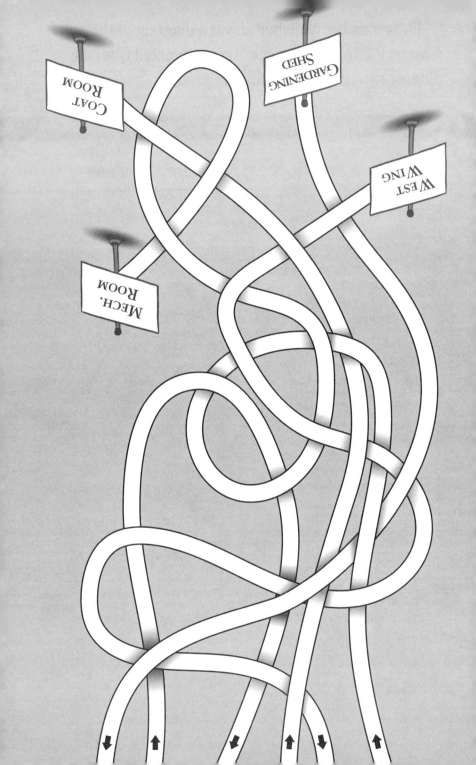

Jayden hoped he wasn't too late! He raced back downstairs to the museum entrance. He peered outside through the glass doors and reeled back in shock.

Cross out all the doors that match.
The leftover letters will spell what Jayden saw.

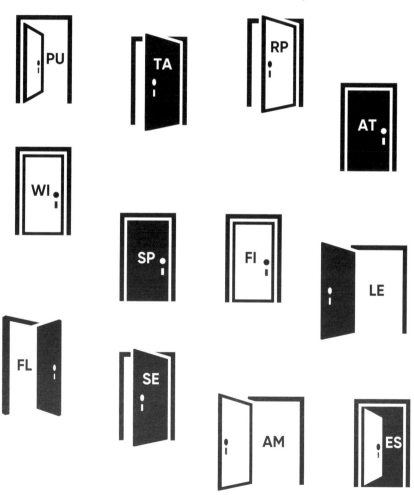

Between museum columns, Jayden could see Chad hovering above the ground inside a ball of purple flame. Chad pounded his fists uselessly against the mystical fire.

Kazzerax stepped into view. There was no trace left of Director Shelley The same purple flames engulfed a giant skeleton! Ancient garments and gold jewelry swung from her bones, glistening.

Quickly, Kazzerax stepped onto a raised symbol, the same one Jayden had seen on the notepad.

She lifted her skull-face to the sky and shouted, "Rise, Architrog, rise!"

Jayden wasn't sure what she was doing, but he knew he had to stop it. He spotted a fire extinguisher next to the entrance doors, pulled it loose, and dashed outside.

He blasted Kazzerax with a cloud of chemicals.

The extinguisher snuffed out Kazzerax's flames. She shrieked and collapsed onto the stone floor with a clatter. At the same time, Chad's fireball fizzled away. He tumbled free, landing hard on his back. Jayden hoisted his friend to his feet.

"Run for it!" Jayden yelled.

The boys dashed down the museum steps. As they reached the bottom, the sky exploded with light. A blinding surge of power hit the museum. Its roof and walls crackled with tentacles of electricity.

"Stop!" Kazzerax bellowed.

Purple flames bloomed around the boys, tossing them into the air.

On fire again, Kazzerax sneered down at them.

"Stick around, boys," she growled. "The Architrog will want a snack!"

"Did she say Architrog?" Chad asked. "What's that?"

"I hope it's a puppy," Jayden answered.

The museum began to shudder and shake. The entranceway cracked open like a pair of jaws. The columns broke in two, becoming rows of jagged teeth.

The window above the entrance fell open to reveal one huge, bloodshot eyeball!

RUMMMMMBLE!

The entire building began to shift and move.

"I... am... alive!" a voice boomed.

Kazzerax rattled down the stairs, grinning wildly.

"I have used the power of the Cosmic Plunger to create an Architrog from this museum!" she announced. "Together, we will rule the world!"

A huge, marble claw reached out from the building and crashed down on Kazzerax.

SKA-CRUNCH!

Bone splinters flew everywhere.

"Puny skeleton," growled the Architrog.

The boys fell to the ground.

"We gotta stop that thing," Jayden said.

"An entire building?" Chad said. "How?"

Look Out!

Are Jayden and Chad doomed?

Is a massive, moving museum about to destroy everything—and everyone—in its path?

We need your puzzling power right now.

Solve this next challenge, and save the world!

HINT:
The answer to the last question can be found on page 26.

"This building, I mean the *Architrog*, must have a weak point somewhere," said Jayden.

"You mean like a heart or brain?" asked Chad.

16   **ARCHI-TROUBLE!**

Answer all the questions. Then follow the dotted line and read the letters in the shaded boxes to answer this question:

WHERE SHOULD JAYDEN AND CHAD GO TO SAVE THE DAY?

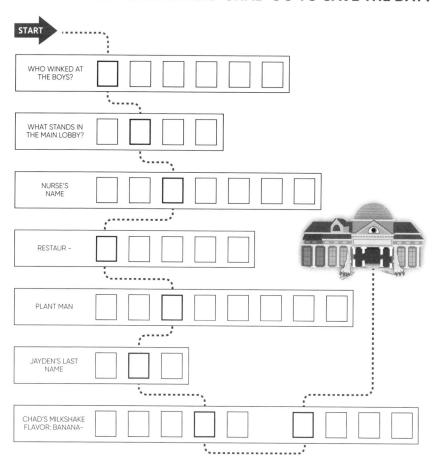

START

WHO WINKED AT THE BOYS?

WHAT STANDS IN THE MAIN LOBBY?

NURSE'S NAME

RESTAUR –

PLANT MAN

JAYDEN'S LAST NAME

CHAD'S MILKSHAKE FLAVOR: BANANA-

DOWN THE DRAIN

"I've got it!" Chad shouted. "The Mech Room. I think it's the brains of the whole museum."

"Works for me," Jayden said. "Let's go."

Claws sprouted from one of the columns. They stretched out above the boys' heads.

"Watch out!" Jayden yelled.

The boys dove out of the way just as the Architrog's claw smacked the ground.

"DESTROY-Y-Y-Y!" the Architrog boomed.

The whole museum started to shift and heave.

"It's going to stand up," Jayden said. "We gotta get in there while we still can."

They sprinted around a corner and spotted an open metal door. They leaped into the building, just as it heaved itself from the ground.

"DESTROY-Y-Y-Y!" the Architrog thundered.

The floor of the museum tilted back and forth like a ship in a storm.

"You sure you want to do this?" Jayden asked Chad.

"I'm done being scared," he said as he toppled into a wall. "Now I'm just mad. That stupid Kazzerax."

The building rose. It felt like riding a crazed, broken elevator. Paintings fell off the wall. Lights flickered and sparked. Beneath them, they heard the Architrog's booming steps. *It was on the move!*

"DESTROY-Y-Y-Y!"

Nurse Jackson dropped through the ceiling and floated in front of them.

"You came back!" she exclaimed. "What do we do?!"

Jayden told her, "Have the monsters meet us in the Mech. Room."

Nurse Jackson saluted and disappeared into the wall.

The boys lurched and tumbled their way through the museum. It was like the world's worst carnival ride. By the time they reached the mechanical room, Jayden felt as if he'd been pummeled with baseballs.

Chad flung open the door. Dazzling light burst from the room. Inside, mystical electricity danced and zipped across the pipes and cables. At the center of it all, a glowing purple shape clung to one of the machines.

"A giant plunger!" Chad shouted.

Nurse Jackson and the other monsters arrived.

"We gotta yank that thing loose," Jayden called to everyone. "But there's so much electricity!"

"I've got this," Shrubley said, stepping forward and wrapping his vines around the handle. "Electricity tickles."

"Make a chain behind Chad and me!" Jayden said, grabbing the plant man around the waist.

Chad and the monsters took hold of each other in a long line. The yeti anchored the end.

"One! Two! Three! *Pull!*" Jayden shouted.

POP!

The plunger came off and disintegrated!

SWOOOOOOOOSH!

The electricity swirled into a glowing purple spiral.

FLUSH!

The hole shrunk into nothingness.

RUM-M-M-MBLE… KA-WHOMP!
The whole building dropped to the ground.

One Week Later

It didn't take long to get to the Supernatural History Museum anymore. After Jayden and Chad had helped remove the mystical plunger, the building returned to normal and ended up two miles away in a much better location!

Even though the monsters were now free to leave, the museum was like home to them. They wanted to stay and run the place. The publicity about a magically moving museum had been great for business!

When the boys returned, the monsters gave them a hero's welcome. Nurse Jackson gave each of them an ice-cold kiss on the cheek and a certificate. It was for one Supernatural Burger and a side of fries.

"That's it… this is the thanks we get?" asked Jayden. "We save the *whole world* and…"

"Shhh," Chad stopped him. "I'm hungry. Let's eat."

You Did It!

The Architrog has been stopped, Kazzerax has been crushed, and the monsters are all back in their places. And, with a newly improved location, the museum is back in business again.

We couldn't have done it without your puzzling power and super solving skills.

Now, there isn't much left to say, but...

Hooray for Puzzlooies!
Big, fun adventures for you.
Excitement and action
For you to peruse,
With a story in the middle
Of the riddles and clues.

You solved a Puzzlooey.
It's over, it's finished, it's through.
And if a scary museum,
Didn't make you screa-um,
There's another one waiting for you!

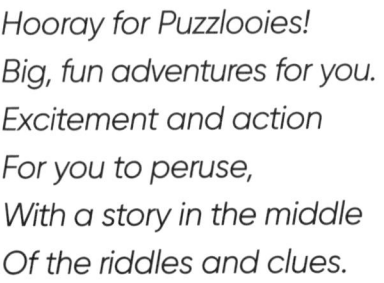

For more smart
and silly fun, go to
puzzlooies.com

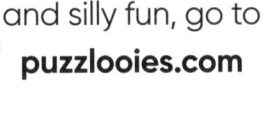

ANSWERS

1 **BEAST OF BOTH WORLDS**

ABOMINABLE SNOWMAN

2 **FEATURED CREATURES**

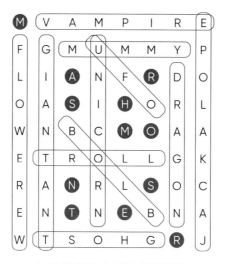

MARSH MONSTER

3   PEEK A BOO

SHE WINKED

4   LETTER BE KNOWN

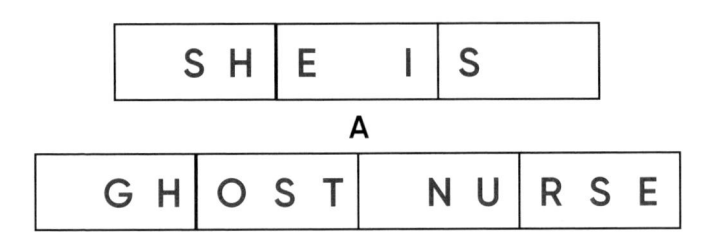

SHE IS A GHOST NURSE

5   WORST AID KIT

WERE-WARTS
ZOMBIE ZITS
WITCH'S BREW-SES

6   A CHANGE OF ART

A HAND IS REACHING OUT TO HIM

8   FRAME-US LAST WORDS

THE NURSE FLEW FROM THE PAINTING

9   DANGER DASH

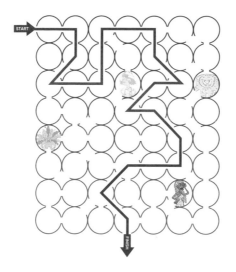

10   CURE GONNA GET IT

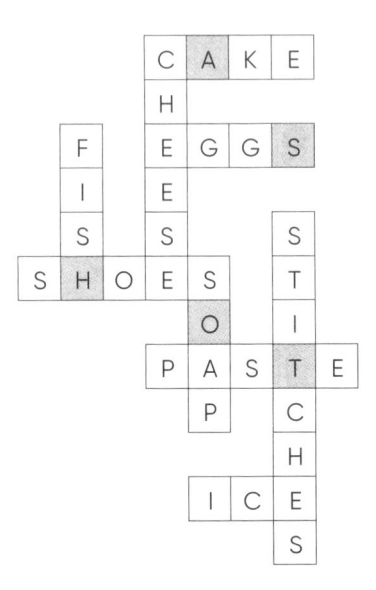

A SHOT

11   BIG SHOT

SWIRLING THOUGHTS

FAINT

SCRAWL OF THE WILD

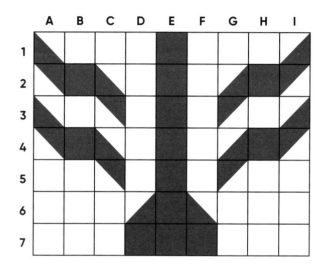

14 **CAN M'YOU SEE 'EM?**

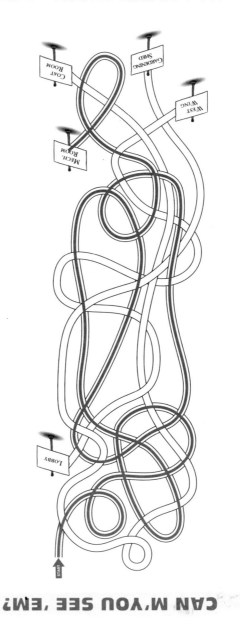

15 **YOU'RE A-DOOR-ABLE**

PURPLE FLAMES

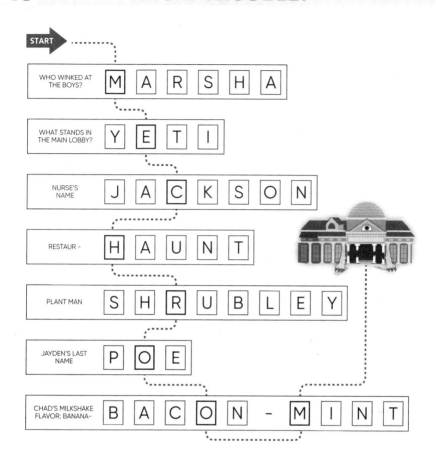

START

| WHO WINKED AT THE BOYS? | M | A | R | S | H | A |

| WHAT STANDS IN THE MAIN LOBBY? | Y | E | T | I |

| NURSE'S NAME | J | A | C | K | S | O | N |

| RESTAUR - | H | A | U | N | T |

| PLANT MAN | S | H | R | U | B | L | E | Y |

| JAYDEN'S LAST NAME | P | O | E |

| CHAD'S MILKSHAKE FLAVOR: BANANA- | B | A | C | O | N | - | M | I | N | T |

MECH ROOM

THEY'RE SMART! THEY'RE FUNNY! TELL YOUR PARENTS TO GIVE YOU MONEY FOR MORE...

PUZZLOO!ES

COLLECT THEM ALL!

To learn more about the other zany, brainy adventures, visit: